GOD *is in the*
little
things

MW01017198

A Child's Song

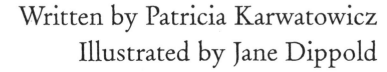

FaithKidz®
Equipping Kids for Life

An Imprint of Cook Communications Ministries
Colorado Springs, CO

Faith
Parenting
Guide
Ages
4-7
Faith

A Faith Parenting Guide
can be found starting on page 32

Written by Patricia Karwatowicz
Illustrated by Jane Dippold

Faith Kidz is an imprint of Cook Communications Ministries
Colorado Springs, Colorado 80918
Cook Communications, Paris, Ontario
Kingsway Communications, Eastbourne, England

A CHILD'S SONG ©2005 by Patricia Karwatowicz

First printing, 2005
Printed in India.
1 2 3 4 5 6 7 8 9 10 Printing/Year 08 07 06 05

ISBN 0781441161

Editor: Heather Gemmen
Design Manager: Nancy L. Haskins
Illustrator: Jane Dippold
Designer: Sandy Flewelling

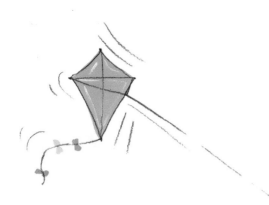

To my grandchildren,
that they may know God loves them
even more then I do.
PK

For Chris, my best friend
JD

"Jesus loves me this I know for the Bible tells me so,"
sang Vivian as she hop-skipped twenty-two jumps on her jump rope.

A new boy in the apartment upstairs
came down the street pushing a wheel.

"Hi," said Vivian. "I'm Vivian. What's that?"

"I'm Tony, and this is Grandpa's old toy," he called as he whizzed past.
"You have to keep it wheeling or it'll fall split-splat!"

Vivian hop-skipped behind him,
singing, "Jesus loves me..."
Tony stopped and stared at the sidewalk.
"Nobody loves me.
Except Grandpa—and he died..."

And he turned to walk away.

"That's not true," called Vivian.
"I'll prove it to you!"

That night she printed a note
with her marker:

Vivian followed a spicy tomato-y aroma
wafting from an upstairs window
and taped the note to the wheel by the door.
She ran downstairs.

The next morning Vivian was on her forty-second jump
when Tony appeared on the steps.

"Thanks, JGV!" he called. "Do you want to trade toys?"
Tony huffed and puffed ten jumps;
he was new at jumping.

Vivian whizzed two wheelies;
she was better at jumping.

11

A man appeared
on the steps.

"Hi,"
she called.
"I'm Vivian."

"Mr. Woo," he said, bowing.

Vivian began to sing again. "Jesus loves me this I know—"
But Mr. Woo interrupted.

"It's okay to sing when everything's going great.
But I lost my poodle Jack. Nobody loves me like he did."
Mr. Woo shuffled down the street.

"That's not true," called Vivian. "We'll prove it to you!"

That night Tony wrote with Vivian's marker:

Tony said to keep Grandpa on the list because Grandpa loved everyone.

15

They followed a soy sauce-y aroma
wafting from an upstairs window
and pushed the note in the mail slot.

Then they ran downstairs.

16

In the morning Tony whizzed nineteen wheelies.
Vivian hop-skipped thirty-one jumps while she sang,
"Jesus loves me…"

Mr. Woo appeared on the steps. "Everything's going great!" he said.
"I found Jack! And he's not the only one who loves me."
Mr. Woo winked at them. "Thanks, JGTVJ!"

Later, Mr. Woo invited his new friends upstairs to meet Jack, who eagerly bounced out of his bed to meet them.

Tony whizzed
twenty-four wheelies.
Vivian hop-skipped
forty-two jumps, singing,
"Jesus loves me this I know
for the Bible tells me so…"

A little girl wearing a red sari
appeared on the steps.

"Hi!" said Vivian. "I'm Vivian!"
Mr. Woo bowed.
Tony waved.
Jack licked at her sandals.

Tears flowed down the little girl's cheek.
"Nobody loves me in this country—"
and she ran upstairs.

"That's not true,"
called Vivian.
"We'll prove it to you!"

Tony, Vivian, and Jack watched Mr. Woo print with the marker and then tape the note to a big piece of crinkly blue paper:

They followed a sweet curry aroma
wafting from an upstairs window
and set the package by the door.

Then they ran downstairs.

In the morning
Tony whizzed thirty-nine wheelies.
Mr. Woo marched Jack
three times down the sidewalk.
Vivian hop-skipped fifty-one times
while singing, "Jesus loves me…"

A beautiful kite bobbed
from a third story balcony.

The little girl poked her head over.
"Hi! I'm Treena. Thanks JGTVMW & J.
I'll be right down!"

Everyone took turns
jumping and whizzing and marching and flying.
People stopped and watched as the four friends sang,
"Jesus loves you this we know for the Bible tells us so!"

"Let us love one another,
for love comes from God..."
1 John 4:7a

31

A Child's Song

AGES: 4-7

LIFE ISSUE: I want my children to share the love of Jesus.

SPIRITUAL BUILDING BLOCK: Faith

Do the following activities to help your children learn to share their faith.

 SIGHT:

Help your children play a game of "I can make you smile" throughout the day: Your children can look for ways to make someone smile. They might sing "Jesus Loves Me" to a grandparent and look for a smile. Or they could tellfriends a story about Jesus that they learned in Sunday school. Or they might simply smile at others and see who smiles back. Help your children think of how to respond when someone asks them why thye're so happy, such as "Because Jesus loves me—AND he loves you, too!"

A Child's Song

AGES: 4-7

LIFE ISSUE: I want my children to share the love of Jesus.

SPIRITUAL BUILDING BLOCK: Faith

Do the following activities to help your children learn to share their faith.

SOUND:

Encourage your children to use their ears to listen for things that can remind people of Jesus' love. Your children might notice when someone prays before a meal, when someone uses comforting words to a child with a new scrape, or when someone sings a song to Jesus as they go throughout the day. Help your children look for times they could encourage someone by simply saying, "Jesus loves you and so do I."

A Child's Song

AGES: 4-7

LIFE ISSUE: I want my children to share the love of Jesus.

SPIRITUAL BUILDING BLOCK: Faith

Do the following activities to help your children learn to share their faith.

✋ TOUCH:

Help your children think of outdoor activities to do with friends that could be used to share God's love. Your children and friends could trace each others' outline on the sidewalk with chalk. Then your children might say, "God loves you just the way you are—tall or short!" Your children could jump rope while singing "Jesus Loves Me." Your children and a few friends could make a parade for Jesus by marching up and down your front sidewalk while singing a favorite Christian song and playing rhythm instruments.

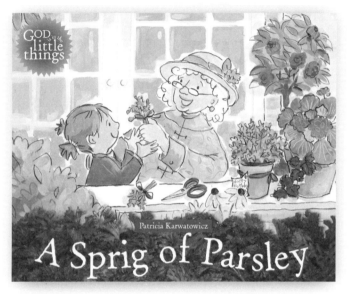

The Word at Work Around the World

What would you do if you wanted to share God's love with children on the streets of your city? That's the dilemma David C. Cook faced in 1870's Chicago. His answer was to create literature that would capture children's hearts.

Out of those humble beginnings grew a worldwide ministry that has used literature to proclaim God's love and disciple generation after generation. Cook Communications Ministries is committed to personal discipleship—to helping people of all ages learn God's Word, embrace his salvation, walk in his ways, and minister in his name.

Faith Kidz, RiverOak, Honor, Life Journey, Victor, NextGen . . . every time you purchase a book produced by Cook Communications Ministries, you not only meet a vital personal need in your life or in the life of someone you love, but you're also a part of ministering to José in Colombia, Humberto in Chile, Gousa in India, or Lidiane in Brazil. You help make it possible for a pastor in China, a child in Peru, or a mother in West Africa to enjoy a life-changing book. And because you helped, children and adults around the world are learning God's Word and walking in his ways.

Thank you for your partnership in helping to disciple the world. May God bless you with the power of his Word in your life.

For more information about our international ministries,
visit www.ccmi.org.